THE
Not-So-Brave
KNIGHT

By Kay Woodward

Illustrated by Yuliya Somina

W
FRANKLIN WATTS
LONDON•SYDNEY

CHAPTER ONE
Arise, Sir Billy!

Once upon a very long time ago, in a castle on a hill, there lived a boy called Billy. He was just like any other boy ... until his twenty-first birthday. On that day, the king called him to the Great Hall.

"Kneel!" commanded King Harold, brandishing his sword. Trembling with fear, Billy did as he was told. But the king didn't chop off his head or challenge him to a sword fight.

He just tapped Billy on each shoulder
with the sword.

"Arise, Sir Billy!" he said grandly.

Trumpets blew and all the other knights
and the ladies-in-waiting cheered politely.

All except Princess Olive, who punched
the air instead.

"Splendid stuff," said King Harold, taking a heavy parcel from Queen May and handing it to him.

"Now, take a good look at this. It'll tell you everything you need to know."

Brand-new Sir Billy unwrapped a huge
book. "How to Be A Knight" said the
fancy letters on the cover.
"Brilliant," he thought. "Now I'll know
exactly what to do."

He took the book to the orchard, where he
sat in the shade of an apple tree. He turned
to the first page and began to read.
"Knights are fair," said the book.
"Great," said Sir Billy, who hated it when
people cheated at chess.

"Knights are loyal," the book said next.
"That's me," said Sir Billy, who would
never let a friend down.

"Knights are polite and obedient and truthful and honourable and faithful and respectful," the book went on, and on. "I'm all of those things," said Sir Billy, ticking them off. "Phew. Being a knight is easy."

Then he turned the next page – and gulped.

"But most of all," said the book, "knights

are brave. The one thing that they never,

ever, ever do is turn down a challenge."

"Oh dear," said Sir Billy. "This could be

a problem."

Because, the thing is, Sir Billy wasn't brave at all. Not even a little bit. He hated sword fights, even as a young boy. Every time the children had played at jousting, knocking each other off make-believe horses with a big stick, he'd run the other way.

Still, there hadn't been a war or a royal tournament for years. No one would ever find out that he was a not-so-brave knight.

"Hey, guess what?" said Princess Olive, sliding to a halt beside the apple tree. "There's to be a tournament next week, with proper jousting and everything. All knights are to take part ."

"Oh, bother," said Sir Billy, "I forgot about the tournament. I mean …

HURRAY!"

CHAPTER TWO
The Royal Tournament

The day of the royal tournament dawned, bright and fair. Sir Billy awoke. He sat up in bed and checked to see if he had magically managed to become brave overnight.

No. His stomach felt as if there were a hundred frogs trapped inside. He took a deep breath. Perhaps the tournament wouldn't be as scary as he feared.

It wasn't – it was scarier. The tournament
ground was a huge rectangular field.
Chattering crowds gathered on each side.

Fluttering flags flew. In the middle were
fearsome knights from other kingdoms.
Every single one of them looked as
if 'Brave' was their middle name.

Sir Billy clanked across the field in his new suit of armour. It had been the last one in the armour shop and it was two sizes too big for him.

16

Meanwhile, Ginger his horse was two sizes

too small. When Sir Billy sat in the saddle,

his feet touched the ground. (But he was

secretly quite pleased about this – at least

he didn't have far to drop when he fell off!)

"Yoohoo!" said Princess Olive, waving

merrily from the grandstand.

"H-h-hi," stuttered Sir Billy, stepping

out of the way as a knight sped past,

riding bareback.

"How do you warm up?" asked a knight

who was doing press-ups.

"Er ... by sitting near the fire?" said Sir Billy.

"Hilarious!" the knight guffawed, switching

to star jumps.

Peowwww! Another knight galloped past. He was standing on his horse's back, riding it like a surfboard. Then another knight cantered by carrying two lances, one in each hand. By now, Sir Billy was shaking so much that his armour rattled like a bag of nails.

A trumpeter played a tune to announce the arrival of King Harold and Queen May. "We shall now decide who will joust against whom!" the king roared, plucking off his crown and presenting it to the queen. She plunged her hand inside and pulled out a paper slip.

"Sir Mark of Wakefield versus ..."

Queen May announced, before sticking

her hand back inside the crown again.

Everyone gasped. Sir Mark was feared by

all. It was rumoured that the ferocious

knight knocked sixty jousters off their

horses every single day (including

twelve before breakfast).

Sir Billy swallowed nervously.

Queen Mary pulled a face.

"Oh dear," she said. "That doesn't seem fair. But it's the luck of the draw so I'm delighted to say that Sir Mark's opponent will be … Sir Billy!"

CHAPTER THREE
A Fierce knight

Sir Billy sat on Ginger, wobbling like a jelly.

At the far end of the tournament ground he

could see his opponent waiting. Sir Mark's

great horse pawed the ground. Sir Mark

was waving at the cheering crowd.

"Ready … steady … GO!" cried King Harold.

Sir Billy lowered his lance and shook

the reins. Ginger began to trot.

"Can you go a little faster?" whispered Billy.

Ginger neighed, blew a raspberry and

carried on at the same speed. Meanwhile,

Sir Mark was galloping towards them.

Sir Mark was travelling faster and faster and getting bigger and bigger. The ground actually shook. Sir Billy felt very nervous indeed. Every single person in the kingdom was here. Soon they would all know how much of a coward he was. What would the crowd do when Sir Mark knocked him off his horse? Would everyone laugh?

And that's when Sir Billy had a brilliant idea. What if he made everyone laugh … ? So Sir Billy trotted onwards. He stared right at Sir Mark, his gaze steady. And at the very last moment, he flung his lance aside. He lunged sideways in the saddle and – wheeee! – rolled under his horse.

Then he carried on riding across the tournament ground, upside down.

Sir Mark thudded past, his lance pointing dead ahead. But he jousted into thin air. The fierce knight stopped and scratched his head. "Where did he go?" he said, shielding his eyes from the sun.

The crowd roared with laughter. They pointed at Ginger and her upside-down rider, nudged their neighbours and clutched their sides.

Finally, Sir Mark
spotted Sir Billy.
He went red.
He went purple.
His eyes bulged. Then he let out
a great bellow of laughter.

"Hysterical!" he cried.
"You win, Sir Billy!" announced
King Harold, who was laughing so much
that tears ran down his cheeks.

"Congratulations!" said the queen.

"Next you will be jousting against ..."

"I hope it's not Sir Jonathan of St Albans," whispered Sir Billy to himself. Sir Jonathan was as strong as an ox. He was rumoured to eat 36 eggs and seven chickens every single day, to build up his muscles.

"... Sir Jonathan of St Albans!" Queen May smiled. Oh no. He was doomed.

CHAPTER FOUR
Scary with a capital S

"Ready … steady … GO!" cried King Harold.
For the second time, Sir Billy shook the reins
and broke into a trot. He squeezed with his
knees to make Ginger go faster. Ginger
ignored him.

In the distance, Sir Jonathan loomed ever larger. His armour was black; his visor was down. He was scary with a capital S. "I'm coming to get you!" roared Sir Jonathan. His horse's hooves drummed the ground. He didn't bother waving at the crowd. His eyes – behind the visor – were fixed on his opponent.

Sir Billy held on tight to the reins and watched the crowd as he trotted slowly past. Everyone was willing him to win. They whooped. They cheered. He gulped. He had been lucky in the last round. He'd made everyone laugh so much that they hadn't realised he was not so brave. But he couldn't get away with it a second time, could he?

"Wow!" Sir Billy shouted, pointing over Sir Jonathan's shoulder. "Look at that! It's the biggest one I've ever seen! UNBELIEVABLE."
"What?" said Sir Jonathan. He turned round in his saddle to look.

His lance whipped round to the side. And as he charged past, Sir Billy ducked neatly beneath it. The crowd went wild. Sir Billy had done it again. He'd survived the joust!

Sir Jonathan lifted his visor and smiled.

"Nice one," he said, shaking Sir Billy's hand.
"Very funny."

"Congratulations, Sir Billy!" said King
Harold, shaking with mirth. "I'm delighted to
tell you that you're through to the final.
Your opponent is Sir Andrew of Nuneaton."

Oh no. This was bad, very bad. It was said that Sir Andrew had so much stamina he could dance for 48 hours, non-stop. Sir Billy would stand no chance against him in a joust.

"Ahem," added the king, pulling a serious face. "No tricks this time, OK? The winner actually has to joust the loser off their horse. And just to make it extra exciting, the winner will win Princess Olive's hand in marriage."

"Eh?" said Princess Olive. "But who says I want to get married!" Billy gulped. Now he was really in trouble. He had to win the next joust to save Princess Olive. And he had to do it properly. But how could he, when he didn't have a smidge of bravery in him? This time, he really was doomed.

CHAPTER FIVE
Doomed!

Sir Billy grasped his lance tightly. He popped his feet into the stirrups. He hung on to the reins. When King Harold gave the signal, he whispered into Ginger's ear. The horse began to trot at once. Then she cantered. And slowly, slowly, she broke into a gallop.

The two knights headed towards each other. Everyone in the crowd held their breath. All the VIPs in the grandstand leaned forward, their eyes glued.

Sir Billy was calm. He watched as Sir Andrew drew closer. The sound of hooves was deafening. The knights lowered their lances.

But at the very last minute, Sir Billy pulled
on Ginger's reins and shouted, "Whoa!"
Sir Andrew skidded to a standstill.

"What is it this time?" he growled.

"I don't know about you," said Sir Billy,
"but I always think these tournaments are
so serious. They could do with cheering up
a bit, don't you think? I mean, before one
of us is knocked off our horse, obviously."

"Um, OK," said Sir Andrew, shrugging.

"Great," said Sir Billy. "I'll start. Why were the Dark Ages called the Dark Ages?"

"I don't know," said Sir Andrew.

"Because there were so many knights!" said Sir Billy. "Get it? Knights? Nights?"

Sir Andrew chuckled.

"Why did the queen visit the dentist?" said Sir Billy.

"I don't know," said Sir Andrew.

"To get her teeth crowned!"

Sir Andrew let out a great, booming laugh.

"And what do you call a knight who works in a hospital?" said Sir Billy.

"I don't know," said Sir Andrew.

"Sir Jen!"

"Ha ha!" said Sir Andrew. "What a terrible joke." He was now laughing so much that all it took was a quick poke of Sir Billy's lance to pop him off the back of his horse. He didn't even notice. He just rolled around on the ground in hysterics.

King Harold wiped his eyes.

"You're the winner, Sir Billy!" he said.

"Smashing," said Sir Billy. "Then do you mind if I don't marry Princess Olive? I think she'd rather like to make her own mind up."

"No problem," said the king.

"Yes!" said Princess Olive, punching the air.

45

Afterwards, everyone said that it was the best royal tournament ever. There wasn't a single injury and no one could remember laughing so much in years.

46

As for Sir Billy, he decided not to joust again. He was still a total coward. And besides, his stand-up comedy routine was in such demand at tournaments around the kingdom that he simply didn't have the time.

Franklin Watts
First published in Great Britain in 2016 by
The Watts Publishing Group

Text © Kay Woodward 2016
Illustrations © Yuliya Somina 2016

The rights of Kay Woodward to be
identified as the author and Yuliya Somina
as the illustrator of this Work have been
asserted in accordance with the Copyright,
Designs and Patents Act, 1988.

Series Editor: Melanie Palmer
Series Advisor: Catherine Glavina
Cover Designer: Cathryn Gilbert
Design Manager: Peter Scoulding

A CIP catalogue record for this book is
available from the British Library.

ISBN 978 1 4451 4993 6 (hbk)
ISBN 978 1 4451 4991 2 (pbk)
ISBN 978 1 4451 4992 9 (library ebook)

Printed in China

Franklin Watts
An imprint of
Hachette Children's Group
Part of The Watts Publishing Group
Carmelite House
50 Victoria Embankment
London EC4Y 0DZ

An Hachette UK Company
www.hachette.co.uk

www.franklinwatts.co.uk

MIX
Paper from
responsible sources

FSC
www.fsc.org

FSC® C104740